Mary Meckler
purpleplumepress@cs.com

The story "Tobias Twissle" is an imprint of Purple Plume Press
Published by Purple Plume Press
5980 Peach Ave
Manteca, CA 95337
Copyright © 2003 Mary Meckler
Manteca, California
All rights reserved.
Printed in Hong Kong

10 9 8 7 6 5 4 3 2 1

Library of Congress Cataloging-in-Publication Data 2003098113
Mary Meckler
The story of "Tobias Twissle"/written by Mary Meckler
Illustrated by Ernie "Hergie" Hergenroeder
Edited by: Janice M. Sellers
Summary: A special man helps a new found friend with encouragement.
ISBN:0-9744923-0-2 (Hardcover)
Copyright to include all characters, design & story concept.

The Magic of
TOBIAS TWISSLE

Nora— Enjoy the magic of Friendship-
Mary Meckler

Written by
Mary Meckler

Illustrated by
Ernie (Hergie) Hergenroeder

Tobias Twissle was a twisted old man
He could have lived in a pretzel can
He stretched and stretched and tried to be tall
Nevertheless, Tobias Twissle shrunk back like a ball.

His legs looked like towels wrung out to dry
His arms were like dowels but dimpled like pie
His neck was quite wobbly; his hair was a fright
Yes, Tobias Twissle was quite a sight.

His twisted legs and twisted arms
Gave him a magical sort of charm,
For his eyes, they sparkled and they glowed
And his smile was never a heavy load.

It seemed that all others who twisted and curved
Felt comfort from this man of great nerve
Tobias Twissle gave his love to all
The short and twisted, the fat and the tall.

It was well known Tobias was a kind, gentle man
The entire town would give him a hand
Whatever was needed, to plow or to sow
His farm was the pride of Twissle Town, you know.

His corn grew so tall, not rangy or lanky
His wheat was the finest, not damp or danky
His house and his barn in the finest repair
Though Tobias Twissle could not walk up a stair.

When Tobias would take a hike down the lane
He walked with a twisted, silly-looking cane
He had no problems walking at all
The cane helped him walk straight;
   It helped him walk tall.

One day Tobias walked into town
He saw a man, quite troubled and down
He tapped his shoulder and said with a smile
"Mind if I sit down for a while?"

The man gave a nod as Tobias sat down
He halfway smiled and tipped his hat off his crown
He squirmed on the curb of the freshly paved street
"Nice to know you," he said,"my name is Pete."

Tobias and Pete, they talked for an hour
Pete could feel Tobias' magical power
As he talked and confessed to his new found friend
His troubles seemed small, his heart did mend.

Tobias then struggled to rise from his spot
His twisted legs would hold him, NOT
Pete jumped to his feet and held out his hand
"Helping each other, it's my pleasure, man..."

It was then that Pete noticed Tobias' twisted frame
And how he walked with the help of a cane
"Well, thanks for the ear," he said with a smile
"I'm glad you sat with me for a while."

"You made me feel on top of the world
my troubles did vanish, my heart did unfurl
I wish I could help you, like you helped me
From your twisted body, I'd like you to be free."

Pete raised his hand to this friend he had found
But Tobias stopped him from making a sound
He smiled and said,"My dear, dear friend,
My body does not need your help to mend."

"My outside is twisted, my looks are a fright
But inside is what matters and inside there's a light
My heart is quite healthy, it beats loud and strong
My friends all know I would never do wrong."

"I care about people and they care about me
Twisted and all, it's my heart that they see."
Then he stretched and he stretched
    and walked away tall
Happy with life, twisted and all.